Contents

1

Trouble at Turtle Bay

I was standing on the deck of the *Wave Dancer*. The sun was shining and I was a happy man. I had no money in my pocket, but the *Wave Dancer* belonged to me.

That morning, she looked like a new boat. Everything was clean and shining. Chubby and Angelo, my crew[1], had done their work well. I had cleaned and checked the two engines. We were ready to leave.

A taxi drove slowly down to the wharf[2]. It stopped and two men got out. One was short with hard, black eyes. The other man was younger and taller. He looked tough. He was trouble.

'Are you Harry Fletcher?' the older man called. He didn't smile.

'That's me,' I replied. 'You must be Mr Materson. Welcome aboard the *Wave Dancer*.'

I took them down to the cabin[3]. It was cool there and very comfortable. The *Wave Dancer* had cost me a lot of money and I looked after her[4] well.

We sat down. 'This is Mike Guthrie,' Materson said.

Guthrie stared at me.

'Don't I know you?' he said. 'You're from London, aren't you?'

'Sure, but I haven't been there for years,' I answered. 'Now, about the fishing,' I went on quickly. 'We'll have to start early tomorrow . . .'

'We're not going fishing, we're going diving[5],' Materson said.

'Pay me well, and you can do whatever you want,' I said with a smile.

4

'*Welcome aboard the* Wave Dancer.'

'All right, then. Here's a list of the things we'll need.'

I looked at the paper Materson had thrown on the table.

'I can get them,' I said.

'Get them by tomorrow, Fletcher. And there'll be three of us. So we won't need your crew.' And Materson looked angrily at Chubby and Angelo.

'Yes, get those two off the boat, fast,' Guthrie added.

'Yes, sir,' I replied. 'You're paying.'

I hated myself for saying that. But I didn't want to lose the job. I needed the money.

'Right. Be ready for us at eight tomorrow morning,' Materson said. 'You alone, remember.'

He threw some money on the table. It was more than I had asked for.

Both men stood up and I watched them go.

⎯⎯⎯

That evening, I was sitting outside my little house among the palm trees at Turtle Bay. I looked across the dark sea to the setting sun. I felt angry and unhappy.

I had lived on St Mary's for five years. It was a beautiful island off the coast of East Africa. My life there had been happy and peaceful. St Mary's was a peaceful island. We didn't want men like Materson and Guthrie on St Mary's. I knew they were bringing trouble.

Guthrie carried a gun and he looked like a killer. Where had he seen me before? In London? Amsterdam? South Africa? He reminded me of my past life. My past life hadn't been peaceful and easy. It had been a hard and dangerous life. It was a life I didn't want to go back to.

2

'He Knew Who I Was'

I ran away from home when I was seventeen and got a job on a ship. Life on board ship was hard and tough, but I loved it. I made money and I spent it fast. Then I became a soldier, fighting other people's wars. I learnt to shoot and kill.

But I never forgot the sea. One day, in the middle of Africa, I decided what I wanted. I wanted to have a boat and a home by the sea. I wanted peace.

But to get these things, I would have to fight once more. To fight for myself this time and break the law[6].

I planned two crimes, the first in London and the second in Amsterdam. Both went wrong, but I escaped. Next, I went to South Africa and worked for a security firm[7]. We moved gold bars all over the world. I worked for this firm for a year. During that time I planned another crime.

This time, I didn't work alone. I got Manny Resnick to help me. We succeeded, we got the gold and I had £150 000 in a Swiss bank account. Then I told Manny Resnick I had finished with crime. But Manny laughed.

'You'll be back, Harry,' he said. 'Let me know when you've planned another job like this one.'

But I didn't go back to crime. I shaved my beard off and bought a false passport[8]. Then I flew to Australia. I bought the *Wave Dancer* there and took her across the seas to St Mary's. I used the rest of the money from the robbery to buy myself some land on the island.

I built a little house between the palm trees and the white sandy beach. There I found the peace I had been looking for.

Now I was sitting in the moonlight, thinking about Materson and Guthrie. I needed the money they had paid me for the use of

Wave Dancer. But did I need the trouble they were bringing?

———

They were at the wharf at 8 am. This time, three men got out of the taxi. The third man was tall and friendly-looking. He was younger than the others and I liked him. I guessed he was the diver.

'This is Jimmy North,' Materson said when they were aboard. 'You will follow his orders.'

'I'm giving instructions, not orders[9],' said Jimmy with a smile. 'When we leave the harbour, travel west.'

'Towards the African coast?' I said. 'The police there don't always welcome strangers.'

'We'll stay offshore[10],' said Jimmy. 'North of the river mouth[11].'

'OK,' I said. 'But it's dangerous. There are police boats and they shoot at strangers. I'll need more money.'

'I thought you would say that,' Materson said softly. 'Just do as Jimmy says and you'll get your money.'

'Are you looking for anything special?' I asked. 'I know these seas. I know every island and every reef[12]. Tell me what you are looking for. I can save you time and money.'

Jimmy laughed excitedly.

'Well,' he said, 'it's the dawn li–'

'Keep quiet,' said Materson. 'What did we tell you? You're here for a job. Just keep your mouth shut while you're doing it.'

Materson went down to the cabin and Jimmy stood beside me on the bridge[13]. Guthrie sat watching us. I could see he had a gun in his pocket.

We found nothing on the first day or the second. On the third day, two things happened. Materson told me he knew who I was. And Jimmy found what they were looking for.

We had just left the harbour and I was alone on the bridge. Materson and Guthrie came up and stood beside me.

'I've been making a few phone calls,' Materson said softly. 'Your name's Bruce, isn't it?'

'Harry Bruce, who did the gold job,' added Guthrie. 'That's who you are – Harry Bruce.'

'Sorry, you've got it wrong,' I said. 'My name's Fletcher.'

'No, you're Bruce,' Materson repeated. 'Harry Bruce disappeared five years ago in Australia. Harry Fletcher arrived in St Mary's harbour three months later. You've done well for yourself, Harry. This is a nice boat. You've got a good life here.'

I said nothing. What could I say?

'Now you listen, Harry Bruce,' Materson said in his soft voice. 'We're looking for something. We need to find it fast. We've decided you can join us. Jimmy can't find the place alone. You help us and we'll keep your secret. We'll forget who you are.' He turned and went down into the cabin.

I stood without moving, staring at the green sea in front of me. When they had found what they were looking for, I guessed they might kill me and perhaps Jimmy too.

Guthrie looked at my face and laughed.

'I'll send Jimmy up,' he said. 'Don't try anything, Harry. You know I've got a gun.'

I thought fast. Jimmy knew the place he was looking for, but he hadn't told the others. Perhaps he also guessed they might kill him. But Materson and Guthrie needed him for the diving. What exactly were they looking for?

The sea off the African coast is full of tiny islands and coral reefs. Many ships have sunk there. Was Materson looking for treasure – gold or beautiful jewels? I began to feel excited. If there was treasure, I wanted my share of it. I began to think hard.

Fishing at Gunfire Reef

Jimmy North came out onto the bridge alone.

'It's OK, Mr Fletcher,' he told me. 'The others have said I can tell you where we want to go. We're looking for an island. It's about ten miles offshore and perhaps thirty miles north of the river.'

'That's a large area of sea, Jimmy,' I said. 'Do you know anything else about this island?'

Jimmy picked up a pencil and made a quick drawing.

'It looks like this,' he said. 'The island has three hills and . . .'

'That's the Old Men,' I said quickly. 'But that island's about twenty miles offshore. And about seventy miles north of the river. We can't get there and back in one day.'

'OK. I'll tell the others,' Jimmy said.

We returned to St Mary's that night, as usual.

Next day, we took enough fuel and food to stay at sea for two days. We reached the Old Men in the afternoon. The island was near Gunfire Reef, a long line of coral facing the open sea.

I steered *Wave Dancer* slowly through the little islands and reefs. It was a dangerous place and I was very careful. We reached the Old Men at last and I anchored[14] in a quiet lagoon. We could hear the noise of the big waves breaking on the outside edge of the reef.

The next morning, after an early breakfast, we started the search again. But Jimmy refused to tell me exactly where we were going. He looked at the three hills and the sea around us over and over again and guided me slowly through the smaller reefs.

After about two hours, we reached the end of Gunfire Reef. Following Jimmy's instructions, I turned into the open sea. We then moved nearer to Gunfire Reef again. We were going south now and the boat moved more strongly in the heavy waves. I looked ahead. The waves were breaking all along the reef. Except in one place. Of course, this was Gunfire Break. Chubby had gone fishing there once and I remembered what he had told me.

'*If you go through Gunfire Break when the tide[15] is high, you're in the deep water behind the first reef. The fish in there are real big, but you can only stay in there for an hour. After high water, the sea pours out from the reef and takes you back with it. There is another way out, through the back of the reef. But that's so dangerous, I don't want to talk about it.*'

'Right,' I called out to Jimmy. 'I'm stopping here. You want to go through the Break, don't you? I guess what you're looking for is in there. But we can't go in there now, the tide isn't right.'

Jimmy said nothing, but he went down to the cabin to talk to the others.

Materson and Guthrie came up to the bridge and Materson began shouting.

'You've had your orders. You do what Jimmy says or we'll tell the police about you.'

I explained the dangers of Gunfire Break. At last, I could see they believed me.

Jimmy came up from the cabin. He was wearing his rubber diving suit.

'I've got an idea,' he said. 'If we can't get through the Break, I want to go along the Reef. I'll use the sledge[16]. We can tow it from the back of the boat.'

While Jimmy was putting on his face mask, I had a good look at the sledge. I had never seen one like it before. The sledge could be pulled along just under the water, or dive down lower. There were special tanks on the sledge to hold air. A diver could lie flat on the sledge and breathe through tubes while he was underwater. There were also steering controls on it. On the side was the name and address of the company who had built the sledge. The address that was written on the side said: "Built by North's Underwater World, 5 Pavilion Arcade, Brighton, Sussex."

Jimmy was now ready.

'If I find anything, I'll send up a yellow marker[17] to the surface,' he said. 'If you see a red marker, that means I'm in trouble. Then you must pull me up – fast!'

'I'll wait for you for three hours,' I said. 'Then I will have to take the *Wave Dancer* away from the reef. The tide will change after three hours. It will be dangerous to stay here after that.'

Jimmy nodded and we lifted the sledge over the side of *Wave Dancer* and into the water. Jimmy lay down on the sledge and took the controls and I began to move *Wave Dancer* along the edge of the reef. The sledge dived below the surface of the water and the rope was pulled tight. I slowed the boat down and I looked back. Jimmy was under the water, and I could see he had moved up to the Break and passed it by.

Then Guthrie gave a shout. He was pointing to a place in the reef near Gunfire Break.

'There's the yellow marker. Jimmy's found something!'

When Jimmy got back on deck, he was very excited. He quickly whispered something to Materson.

Materson turned to me and said, 'OK, Fletcher. Jimmy wants to go down and get it.'

'Get what?' I asked. 'What's he found down there? How big is it?'

'Not very big,' Jimmy said. 'It weighs about 25 kilos. If you can keep the boat steady[18], I'll use air-bags[19] to get it out.' And he pointed back excitedly towards Gunfire Break.

For forty minutes I held the *Wave Dancer* steady. Suddenly I saw the green air-bags. It was time to move away from the Reef.

As we pulled Jimmy onto the deck of *Wave Dancer* again, he began shouting excitedly.

'Materson! It's there! I've found the –'

'Quiet,' said Materson sharply. They all looked at me for a

moment. Then they turned to the object that Jimmy had brought up from the sea. It was lying on the deck. Jimmy had wrapped it in strong cloth and I couldn't see what it was. I was very interested indeed. Then Materson smiled up at me.

'OK, Fletcher,' he said. 'Come and have a look.'

I didn't think anything was wrong. I wanted to know what the object was. I moved quickly down to the deck. Then Materson whispered, 'Now!' and I was looking into the black mouth of Guthrie's gun.

I jumped to one side, but I was too late. There was a sharp pain and a loud noise. A bullet had hit me in the chest. I fell against the rail of the boat and then I was falling. Falling, falling, into the clear green sea . . .

4

Murder!

I could not breathe. I wanted air, but I dared not go up to the surface. I knew that if I swam up to the surface, Guthrie would shoot again. I opened my eyes and began to move slowly as the *Wave Dancer* passed above me.

Then everything went dark. The sea was red with blood – my blood. I could not move my left arm and I needed air. I had to go up!

I saw a rope from the *Wave Dancer* hanging down into the water. I caught it with my right hand, held on to it and pulled myself up, under the stern of the boat.

I had only one chance – to get to the automatic rifle in the cabin. I had to get it before Materson and Guthrie saw me.

Up! Up! With one last pull, I dragged myself up onto the deck. I lay there and looked down at my body. Blood was pouring out of my arm and chest. My legs were weak and my mind was not clear. Then I heard Jimmy North shouting from the bow of the boat.

'You murderers! You've killed him! I'm going down there to get his body. You'll be hanged for this!'

Jimmy turned away and pulled on his face mask. I saw

14

Materson look at Guthrie and I tried to shout. Guthrie moved up to Jimmy, put the gun to his head and fired.

Jimmy was dead. With a splash, his body fell into the water.

'He'll sink,' said Materson. 'He was wearing lead weights on his belt. But we must find Fletcher's body.'

I knew then that I had to kill both of them. Slowly, I dragged myself across the deck and down into the cabin.

'Ten seconds, please God! Give me ten seconds!' I whispered.

Now the heavy gun was in my hands, but I could not hold on to it. It crashed to the floor.

'Come on!' I heard Materson cry. 'There's someone in the cabin. Fletcher's down there. You didn't kill him. Look! There's blood all over the deck!'

I picked up the rifle again and pointed it towards the cabin door. It felt very heavy and I could hardly see.

Materson ran into the cabin and fired once. I fired back, and his body was thrown across the cabin. There was more blood in the cabin now – Materson's blood. But I went on firing.

Then Guthrie was outside the cabin. He put his hand round the door and fired once. I fired back and was lucky. My last bullet hit him in the arm and his gun was thrown across the deck.

We stared at each other. Materson's dead body lay between us. I began to move slowly towards Guthrie. He reached out to pick up his gun. There was no way I could stop him.

Then a huge wave hit the boat. The *Wave Dancer* rose up and up and the gun fell from Guthrie's hand. He went after it, slipped in the blood on the deck and fell heavily.

Suddenly, I remembered the knife in my belt. It was my last chance. Guthrie had his back towards me now. I stood up slowly and threw the knife with all my strength. Guthrie gave one loud scream and then lay still. When I turned him over, his dead eyes stared up at me. I lay on the deck and everything went black.

I woke up six hours later. The hot sun had burned me. There was a terrible pain in my chest. Guthrie's bullet had gone through my arm and chest and torn a hole in my back. I was still bleeding badly.

I dragged myself back into the cabin. I washed my wounds and covered them. I found some cold water and drank and drank. I had enough strength to start the *Wave Dancer's* engines. There was no land in sight.

I set the automatic pilot on a course[20] for St Mary's. Then I fell back onto the deck and once again everything went black. When I woke up, the sun was setting. There was land ahead – Gull Island. I had gone past St Mary's but I was near home.

I looked at the object on the deck that Jimmy North had brought up from the sea. It was still wrapped up and tied with strong rope. I could not guess what it was. But I knew that three men had already died because of it. I wanted to open the bundle[21]. I wanted to see what was inside. But I was getting weaker and weaker.

I decided to push the bundle overboard and come back for it later. I looked carefully towards Gull Island. I had to remember exactly where I was. Then, with the last of my strength, I pushed the bundle along the deck and over the side.

My wounds had begun to bleed again. I fell back on the deck and slept until the morning sun woke me.

Chubby found me. He had gone fishing in his old whaleboat[22] with Angelo. He called my name and I opened my eyes. But I was too weak to answer him.

5

Sherry's Story

I had to stay in hospital for nearly a month. The police came many times to ask me questions. I did not tell them anything about the bundle in the sea near Gull Island. But I thought a lot about Jimmy and why he had died. I had liked him. He had died because he tried to help me.

The President of St Mary's came to see me. He was a good friend of mine. He smiled at me as I lay in the hospital bed.

'Now, don't worry, Mr Harry,' he said. 'There'll be no trouble for you. The people you killed were real bad men. The police in England know all about them. These men came here to make trouble. If you hadn't killed them, they would have killed you.

'Don't worry, Mr Harry. You get well as soon as you can. You must come to dinner with me very soon. I want to hear the whole story again . . .'

There were no more visits from the police after that. Chubby and Angelo came to see my every day. Angelo's girlfriend, Judith, sometimes came too. Her pretty face helped me to get better fast!

Judith worked as a receptionist at the Hilton Hotel where the tourists stayed. If they wanted to hire a boat to go fishing, Judith gave them my name.

When I left hospital, I had to rest. I drove in my truck to my house in Turtle Bay. I swam and rested in the sun. Slowly, my body grew hard and strong again. But I had bad scars[23] on my chest and my left arm was still stiff and weak.

The fishing season[24] had finished and I needed money quickly. I had to pay Chubby and Angelo's wages and *Wave Dancer* had to be repaired. One way to get money quickly was to smuggle[25] goods across to the African coast. For six weeks, the three of us, Chubby, Angelo, and myself, made the trip to Africa. We grew rich.

I hadn't forgotten the bundle under the water. I knew I would go back to Gull Island one day, but not yet.

One night, I was sitting in a bar with Chubby and Angelo, when Judith came in.

'There's a lady at the hotel asking for you, Mr Harry,' she said.

'A lady? Who is this lady?' I said.

'I don't know,' said Judith, 'but she's asking for you and she's beautiful.'

———

I went up to the hotel next morning. Judith was at her desk and she smiled at me.

'She's waiting for you outside by the swimming pool. She's a blonde lady and she's wearing a yellow bikini.'

The girl was lying by the pool, reading a magazine. When she heard me, she turned and sat up.

She had a lovely body and long blonde hair. Her make-up made her pretty face smooth and beautiful. I walked towards her with the smile I give to all pretty women.

'Hi!' I said. 'I'm Harry Fletcher.'

She looked at me and smiled.

'Hallo, Harry,' she answered. 'I'm Sherry North – Jimmy's sister.'

———

That evening, as we sat outside my little house, we talked about Jimmy. Sherry showed me a letter in Jimmy's handwriting. Jimmy's words were full of life and excitement. I remembered how much I had liked Jimmy.

'OK,' I said. 'You're Jimmy's sister. You've come to St Mary's to see me. Why?'

She answered me with a question.

'You liked Jimmy, didn't you?' she said.

'I like a lot of people,' I replied. 'Perhaps I like too many people.'

19

'Did Jimmy tell you what he was doing out here?' she asked.

I shook my head. 'No. And I never ask questions.'

Sherry looked at me.

'Jimmy liked you,' she said quietly. 'And he trusted[26] you. I need your help now. I'm going to trust you too.'

Sherry moved closer.

'Two years ago, there was a terrible storm here – a cyclone. Do you remember it?'

'Of course I do. It did a lot of damage.'

'Well,' Sherry went on, 'when the cyclone began, an American war-plane was flying near here. It was carrying four nuclear missiles. The plane crashed in the sea. The pilot escaped, but the missiles sank in the sea with the plane.'

'What has Jimmy to do with this?' I asked.

'The pilot of the plane was Jimmy's friend. His name was William Bryce. He was rescued. They searched for the missiles, but never found them. The missiles are still under the sea. Because of the accident, Bryce lost his job. But he never told anyone that he knew where the missiles were.'

I started to ask a question, but Sherry went on.

'Bryce made a plan. With Jimmy's help he would get the missiles up. Then he would sell them back to the Americans.'

'Those missiles would be worth millions,' I said slowly. 'Go on, I'm very interested.'

'Of course, Bryce and Jimmy needed money and people to help them. Then Bryce was killed in a car accident. Jimmy found people to help him, but they were the wrong kind of people. Poor Jimmy! You know the rest of the story.'

'I know the rest,' I said. 'I know everything – except where the missiles went down.'

A look of anger passed over Sherry's face. We stared at one another.

'Didn't Jimmy tell you where the missiles went down?' I asked.

She shook her head. Tears came into her eyes.

'Well, that's that,' she said. 'I've come a long way to find you. Jimmy trusted you. I thought we could work together. But if you want all the money yourself, I can't do anything about it . . .'

'Perhaps I can do something about it,' I replied.

6

Explosion!

Sherry North was beside me when I took the *Wave Dancer* out of St Mary's harbour the following afternoon. I didn't trust Miss Sherry North and I had done a lot of thinking.

The object in the bundle that Jimmy had brought up from the sea was not a missile. It was the wrong shape. But I was taking Sherry North to Gull Island. I wanted to see what she would do.

We found the place easily.

'This is it,' I said. 'This is where Jimmy dived. When he came up, he was very excited. That's when the shooting started.'

'Yes,' she said, 'that's why we must go now – before someone sees us.'

'Go?' I repeated in surprise. 'No, I'm going down to get it. I didn't come here for nothing.'

I went below deck to get into my rubber diving suit. But before I came up on deck, I switched off the electrical power. Now she couldn't start *Wave Dancer's* engines.

I put on my face mask and moved slowly down the ladder into the water. The water was very clear and I could see the bundle sixteen metres below me. I fastened a rope to it and swam back to the surface. I got back onto the deck and slowly pulled the bundle up from the bottom of the sea.

When the bundle was on the deck, Sherry looked at it greedily.

'Open it, Harry, open it,' she said.

I began to untie the ropes. At last, I unwrapped the cloth. I was watching Sherry's face carefully. She knew what the object was before I did. For one second, her face was full of excitement. But she quickly hid her excitement and her face went blank. The object on the deck was made of metal, but it had never been part of a missile. It was a ship's bell[27] and it had been under the sea for many years. I turned it over carefully and I could see a crest[28] and the letters WN LI. The rest of the letters had been worn away.

'That's strange,' I said, looking at Sherry. 'Planes don't have bells, do they?' Sherry did not laugh.

'I don't understand,' she said. She tried to speak calmly, but I could see she was very excited.

'This is what Jimmy found. This is what three men died for,' I said. 'I think I'll go down and look around.' I did not tell Sherry that this was not where Jimmy had found the bell. He had found it far away at Gunfire Reef.

'No, no,' Sherry said quickly. 'Let's go back. I feel seasick[29]. Take me back, Harry.'

I wrapped the cloth and tied the ropes round the bell again.

'First of all, this is going back under the water. It'll be safer there.'

'OK,' said Sherry, 'but then let's get back as quickly as we can. I think I'll go and make you some coffee.'

Sherry went into the cabin, but came back almost at once.

'The stove[30] won't light,' she said.

'You have to open the taps on the gas-cylinders first,' I told her. 'And remember to turn them off when you've finished. If you don't, the boat will be as dangerous as a bomb.'

*It was a ship's bell and it had been under the sea
for many years.*

It was dark when we reached Sherry's hotel.

'Darling, I'm tired,' she said. 'I want to go to bed now. We can talk tomorrow, on the boat.'

'OK,' I said. 'What time shall I pick you up here tomorrow?'

'Don't come here. I'll meet you on the boat – about eight o'clock.'

'OK. I'll bring the *Wave Dancer* up to the wharf at eight,' I agreed.

On my way home, I saw Angelo and Judith in the bar.

'Harry, come and have a drink,' Angelo called. 'How are you getting back home tonight?'

'In the truck, of course. Why? Do you want to borrow it?'

'Can we borrow it just for tonight, Mr Harry, please?' said Judith. 'There's a big party in the village. Angelo will pick you up in the morning, I promise.'

'OK,' I said. 'Take me home now. Then you can pick me up at seven tomorrow morning.'

I had bad dreams that night. In the morning, Angelo arrived on time and I drove him back to St Mary's. Something was worrying me, but I didn't know what it was.

'Judith's gone to the boat to tidy it up for you,' Angelo said. 'She's going to get the coffee ready.'

I didn't answer. Instead of going straight to the wharf, I took the road up to the Hilton Hotel.

'Is Miss North in her room?' I asked the girl at the desk.

'Miss North?' she repeated in surprise. 'She left for the airport an hour ago. She'll be on the 7.30 plane by now.'

It didn't make sense. Then suddenly I understood.

'Oh, my God, Judith!' I shouted.

I ran back to the truck and drove off as fast as I could.

'What is it, Mr Harry?' Angelo asked.

'We've got to stop Judith. She mustn't go on the *Wave Dancer*,' I shouted.

But it was market-day and the streets were full of people. It took too long to get to the wharf.

I stood looking out across the sea. Judith was in a small boat. She had just reached the *Wave Dancer*. I shouted as she went down into the cabin, but she couldn't hear me. She was too far away. I knew what was going to happen. Sherry North had planned it all!

There was a bright blue flash and a terrible explosion. The *Wave Dancer* was lifted out of the water, fell and disappeared.

I had never felt so angry. Sherry had meant to kill me. Instead, she had destroyed my boat and murdered a beautiful young girl.

I had lost my boat and Angelo had lost Judith. Both our lives had been changed in a few terrible seconds.

7

Sherry North Again

We saved a few things from the *Wave Dancer*, including my automatic rifle. But that was all.

I had insured *Wave Dancer* with a local insurance agent[31]. But I soon found out he had been cheating me. He had taken my money, but hadn't insured the boat. So I couldn't get any money at all.

No boat – no job. Harry Fletcher was back where he had started.

I had to find the blonde girl called Sherry North. I had never trusted her. Now I was sure she wasn't Jimmy North's sister. But who was she? And what did she want? Why had she been so excited when she had seen the ship's bell? And why had she told so many lies?

I started to think about that ship's bell. Many old ships had been wrecked on the dangerous coral reefs. Had Jimmy found out about a ship full of treasure that had sunk near Gunfire Reef? If he had, then the girl called Sherry North knew about it too. If there were gold and jewels in the ship, I wanted my share of them.

I asked a few questions at the hotel. The night before she

left, the blonde girl had sent a cable. It had been addressed to someone called Manson in London. I had enough money left to get to London. I would find the girl and the man called Manson there, if I was lucky. And I also had another clue – an address in Brighton. I remembered what had been written on the side of Jimmy's sledge. I decided to go there first. There might be notes, maps, anything in Brighton. I had to find that treasure! I bought a ticket for the next plane leaving St Mary's.

England was cold and wet. I hired[32] a car at the airport and drove to Brighton. It was dark when I found Jimmy's shop. The shop was closed, but there was a notice on the door: "Enquiries to Seaview, Downers Lane, Falmer, Sussex."

I drove to Falmer and found the cottage called Seaview. There was a light shining from one of the windows. Someone was in there. But who? Was I too late? I parked my car and walked quietly over to the door. I knocked and waited.

A girl opened the door, but it wasn't the blonde. This girl was very tall, with dark hair and blue eyes. Her skin was pale and clear. She was very beautiful. We stared at one another and then she said, 'You're Harry Fletcher.'

'How do you know that?'

'Come in and I'll tell you,' she answered.

We stood in the kitchen looking at each other.

'There was a report in the papers about the trouble at St Mary's,' the girl explained. 'Your picture was in the papers, with Jimmy's. That's how I knew your name.'

'But I don't know yours,' I said slowly.

'I'm Sherry North,' she said.

'You're the second Sherry North I've met,' I said with a smile.

She was very different from the other girl and I liked what I saw. I decided to trust her.

'I will tell you the whole story,' I said.

She was a stranger, but I told her everything. I told her about Jimmy and the other men. I told her about the blonde girl. I told her everything about myself – the good and the bad. Perhaps I was stupid, but I could not help it. It was midnight when I had finished speaking. But I still had a question to ask her.

'Why exactly did Jimmy go to St Mary's?' I said.

'I don't know, but I'll help you find out,' the girl replied. 'We'll talk again in the morning. You can sleep in Jimmy's room tonight.'

I fell asleep almost at once. I woke up sometime later. Someone was speaking very quietly downstairs.

I got out of bed and walked to the top of the stairs.

Sherry North was on the phone, talking quickly and quietly. Why? But I was too tired to think any more. I went back to bed and slept until morning.

After breakfast we sat together in the kitchen. Sherry told me what she knew. She had known very little about Jimmy's plans. The police had told her about his death.

'Who were the people who killed Jimmy?' she asked me. 'And what was Jimmy looking for?'

'What do you think Jimmy was looking for?' I asked.

'Well, Jimmy was always interested in treasure,' Sherry said. 'He was always reading about gold and silver found at the bottom of the sea.

'I know there are a lot of files[33] in Jimmy's room,' she went on. 'I haven't looked at them. But perhaps there are some clues in those files.'

I went up to Jimmy's room and took down the big, black files. One of them contained old letters and I looked through them quickly. In the tenth letter I looked at, I found something. Two words – *Dawn Light* – had been underlined in pencil. Where had I heard those words before? Then I remembered that day on the *Wave Dancer*. Jimmy had started to say something but Materson had stopped him. I remembered Jimmy's voice: '*It's the dawn li . . .*'. I understood now. The *Dawn Light* was the name of a ship! I looked at the letter again. Yes, I was right.

In September 1857, the *Dawn Light* had sailed from India with five large boxes on board. What had been in those boxes and where were they now?

Then I remembered the ship's bell and the writing on it . . WN LI . . .. Of course I knew where the boxes were! They were at the bottom of the sea, at Gunfire Reef!

I went on reading Jimmy's files all morning. It was all there – all the information we needed.

The *Dawn Light* had left Bombay for London. On the way, she was going to call at St Mary's. But the ship had been wrecked on Gunfire Reef. It had sunk with everything on board.

Twelve people escaped in a small boat and finally they got back to England. But the *Dawn Light* and everything in it was still at the bottom of the sea.

Sherry and I were very excited. Jimmy's room was full of files and papers. It took us a long time to find what we were looking for. Then Sherry gave an excited cry.

'Look, Harry,' she said, 'look at this.'

She had found a chapter photocopied[34] from a book. The chapter was called "The Tiger Throne of India". We read the words together. I knew at last what Jimmy had been looking for – and what Sherry and I were going to find!

She had found a chapter photocopied from a book.

8

The Tiger Throne

The Tiger Throne had belonged to an Indian prince. It was made of gold and covered with jewels. The gold seat was shaped like a tiger's face – a tiger with one great eye. And in that eye was a huge diamond – the biggest ever found in India.

During the Indian Mutiny[35], the Throne had disappeared. No one knew where it had gone – no one knew until now. The Throne had been stolen by an Englishman. He had broken the Throne into four parts and put the parts into wooden boxes. All the jewels were taken from the Throne and put in another box. It was those five boxes that the Englishman had tried to bring to England on the *Dawn Light* in 1857. But the *Dawn Light* had sunk and only Sherry and I knew where it was! If we could find the ship and raise the boxes, we would be rich for the rest of our lives.

Then I thought about the blonde girl and her friends. They believed that the *Dawn Light* had gone down near Gull Island. But they wouldn't find the treasure there. Then the girl and her friend Manson would start looking for me and Jimmy's sister. They would get the truth from us somehow.

We had to go back to St Mary's quickly. We had to find the treasure before the others found us. I told Sherry my plan.

'I know where the *Dawn Light* went down,' I said. 'We'll go back to St Mary's together. I'll send Chubby a cable. He and Angelo will help us.

'We'll take Jimmy's notes and papers with us. There's an old plan of the ship[36] here. It will help us find the boxes.'

Sherry was as excited as I was. She told me that she was a very good diver.

'Then both of us can go down to find the *Dawn Light*,' I said.

'We can use Chubby's old whaleboat. It's got good engines and it will get us to the Reef.

'You will come with me, won't you?' I asked Sherry. Her blue eyes looked into mine.

'Yes, Harry,' she said. 'We'll finish what Jimmy started. We'll find the treasure together.'

'Perhaps I've found my treasure here,' I said and took her in my arms.

Chubby and Angelo were at St Mary's airport to meet us. We started making our plans that same day. I could see that Chubby and Angelo liked Sherry. I knew we would all get on well together.

Sherry and I left Chubby and Angelo preparing for the journey to Gunfire Reef. I took Sherry with me to Turtle Bay. I wanted to be alone with her.

When Sherry saw Turtle Bay, she was amazed.

'Oh, Harry,' Sherry said softly, 'I didn't think it would be like this. It's beautiful. It's like heaven.'

She smiled at me and her eyes were the colour of the dark-blue sea.

During the time at Turtle Bay, I knew I loved Sherry. Once or twice, I saw a strange look in her eyes. But I took no notice. I loved her and I thought she loved me. I was happier than I had ever been before.

While Sherry and I were at Turtle Bay, Chubby was busy getting the old whaleboat ready. We had saved the diving things from the wreck of the *Wave Dancer*. Chubby bought camping equipment[37], food and everything we needed. We packed the old whaleboat with the equipment and early next day we set off for Old Men Island.

We were going to camp on Old Men Island and go to

Gunfire Reef each day. On the way, Chubby told me more about the narrow channel through the coral at the back of the Gunfire Reef.

'It's dangerous, Mr Harry, very dangerous. But I guess I can get the old boat through safely. If we used that channel, we can save a journey of twenty miles each day. When we are through the channel, we will be in the pool in the middle of the Reef. I guess the *Dawn Light* is down there somewhere.'

'OK, Chubby,' I said. 'You know these reefs better than I do.'

We reached Old Men Island in the late afternoon. We began immediately to move all our equipment onto the beach.

The following day, Chubby went back to St Mary's for more fuel and water. We decided to make our camp up in some caves on the hillside. Angelo and I were busy all day carrying our equipment up to the caves. When all the equipment was stored in the caves I climbed with Sherry to the top of the highest hill. We looked down at the reef.

'How long will it take to find the treasure?' Sherry asked.

'I don't know,' I told her. 'But we can only work in the pool when the tide is right. And I think that the other "Sherry" will be back with her friends soon. We did not have time to find out who they were. But I guess they won't be very nice people.'

'But how will we know when they arrive?' Sherry asked.

'We'll keep in contact with St Mary's,' I told her. 'Chubby's friends will tell us if any strange boats arrive. They'll tell us if the girl comes back again. I wonder who she'll bring with her.'

We sat there in silence, enjoying the peace of the island. I had a feeling that this peace would not last much longer.

9

The Search for Dawn Light

It was dark when Chubby brought the whaleboat back. We carried the new supplies up to the cave. Now it was time to tell Chubby and Angelo exactly why we were there.

The two men listened in silence. Then Chubby took something from his pocket. It was a gold coin. On one side of the coin was the same crest I had seen on the ship's bell.

'Where did you get this, Chubby?' I asked in surprise.

'When I was a boy, I caught a big old fish in the pool at Gunfire Break. When I opened the fish, I found this coin inside. I've kept it ever since.'

'Well, that shows the story is true, Chubby,' I said. 'That old ship must be down there in the pool.'

'If it's there, we'll find it,' Chubby replied with a smile. 'The next high tide's at 1.40 tomorrow.'

The next day, Chubby took us through the narrow channel and into the pool behind the Reef. The channel turned and twisted between the great lumps of sharp coral. Several times, I thought we would hit them, but Chubby got the whaleboat through safely.

'We'll have to keep the engines going,' Chubby told me. 'This pool's too deep for an anchor.'

We had about an hour in which we could work. We had to work fast, so Sherry and I went down together.

The pool was a dark hole beneath us and, as we went down and down, the water got colder.

The coral had grown into a hundred different shapes in a hundred different colours. Small, brightly coloured fish swam all around us. They shone like jewels in the light of our torches.

We went lower and the water grew darker. Now we were swimming in an underwater forest of coral and sea plants.

I looked at my watch. We had been below for about ten minutes. We were at the bottom now. We moved slowly. We were looking for anything which might have come from the *Dawn Light*. When we saw anything unusual, we broke it from the coral and put it in our netting-bags[38].

I looked at my watch again and made a sign to Sherry. It was time to go. We swam up to the surface very slowly. Going up too fast was dangerous and could bring death to a diver. Angelo helped us out of the water. Chubby started the whaleboat moving immediately.

'Just in time, Mr Harry,' he said. 'The tide's turning. We must get out through the channel real fast.'

As soon as we were back on the beach at Old Men Island, we emptied our bags and looked at the objects we had found.

'Here's a key, a small key!' Sherry cried.

In another piece of coral, there was something white. I turned it over in my hand. It was a piece of china plate. There was a blue pattern on it and the same crest that I had seen on the ship's bell.

'It's a piece of a plate,' I said. 'When the ship broke up on the Reef, everything would have poured out of it onto the bottom of the sea. Everything that was in the *Dawn Light* will be there. But everything will be covered in thick coral, like this piece of plate.'

'And the treasure?' Sherry asked. 'What about the treasure boxes?'

We sat in silence for a moment. Then Chubby spoke.

'The boxes will still be on the ship,' he said. 'All the important cargo would be in the front of the ship. This part of the ship would be very strong. Those boxes will still be there.'

'I hope you are right, Chubby,' I said. 'If those boxes fell out of

*When we saw anything unusual, we broke it from the coral
and put it in our netting-bags.*

the ship, they'll be at the bottom covered with coral. We'll never find them.'

I thought quietly, then said, 'There are two things we've got to do. First, we've got to find those boxes – and be sure they are the right ones. Then, we've got to get them out of the coral.'

'We'll need explosives[39], Mr Harry. We'll have to blow up that old coral,' Chubby said.

'Can you get some?' I asked.

'Sure, Mr Harry, if you've got the money I can get you anything.'

'Right, we'll get the explosives the next time we go to St Mary's. I've got some business to do there too.'

I noticed that Sherry said very little. She had a strange, cold look on her beautiful face. I was sure now that she had not told me everything about herself. But I didn't want to think about that now.

During the next five days, we went down into the pool every time the tide was right. I wanted to work fast. I had a feeling that trouble was on the way.

When the blonde girl and her friends arrived, they would go to Gull Island. They would find the ship's bell, but nothing else. Then they would start asking questions about Harry Fletcher.

On the fifth day, we found the wreck of the *Dawn Light*. The front part of the ship had been broken off and was lying against the bottom of the reef.

'You were quite right, Chubby,' I said. 'The front part was very strong and hasn't broken apart. But it's lying bottom up and it's covered with thick coral. Come down and have a look.'

'We'll need explosives for sure,' Chubby said when he came up. 'Not too much, just enough to break up the coral.'

'There's a good moon tonight,' I said. 'Can you take us back to St Mary's?' Chubby nodded.

It was after midnight when we reached the wharf. No one saw us arrive. We walked up to Chubby's house and had coffee there.

Then Sherry and I drove on to Turtle Bay.

Sherry fell asleep almost at once. But I had a lot of thinking to do. I wanted three things. I wanted a quiet life on St Mary's. I wanted another *Wave Dancer* and I wanted Sherry North.

To have the first, I had to stay friends with the President of St Mary's. To get the second, I needed a lot of money. And the third? That would have to wait.

10

The Enemies Return

Early the following morning, I drove myself to the President's house. The President was delighted[40] to see me.

'Come in, Harry, my boy,' he said. 'You look well again. What have you been doing since you left hospital?'

I took a deep breath.

'Well, sir,' I said slowly. 'That's what I've come to talk about.'

'Always pleased to talk to you, Harry, my boy,' said the President. 'Stay to lunch.'

It was a long lunch. I had a lot to tell the President and he listened carefully. Then he asked a lot of questions – but in the end, he agreed with my plans.

It was late in the afternoon when I drove back to Turtle Bay. I felt pleased with myself. Everything was OK. The President was on my side.

Chubby had got the explosives. I didn't ask him where he had got them from. I gave him the money he asked for and we put the unmarked boxes onto the truck.

'We need some more food on the island,' I said. 'We'll get the food and load it into the truck. Then you get your whaleboat round to Turtle Bay, Chubby. If anyone asks, say you're going fishing. We'll load everything onto the whaleboat this evening. Then we can sail back to Gunfire Reef at dawn.

'I'm sure that the blonde girl who called herself Sherry North will be back here soon. She's bad news for all of us!'

The bad news came sooner than I thought. Chubby and I were in the store, buying food, when Angelo came in with Sherry.

'Mr Harry,' he called. 'I want to show you something.'

I went outside and looked where he was pointing. A beautiful blue and white ship had just anchored at the entrance to the harbour. There were some people standing on the deck staring at the shore.

'That's trouble,' I said quietly. I looked through my binoculars[41]. The blonde girl who had called herself Sherry North was standing on the bridge. Beside her stood a man I knew immediately although I hadn't seen him for nearly six years. Manny Resnick! So he was Manson. Like me, he had changed his name. And he knew who I was. He knew enough about my old life to put me in prison for years. And now he was in St Mary's, looking for the *Dawn Light* and the Tiger Throne!

'Quick, Chubby,' I said. 'There's no time to lose. We must leave St Mary's tonight. The man on that boat is our enemy. And that's the girl who destroyed *Wave Dancer* and killed Judith!'

'Then I'll be happy to kill them both, Mr Harry,' Angelo said quietly.

'You'll get your chance, Angelo,' I told him, 'if they don't kill us first!

'We've got to get that treasure out of *Dawn Light* quickly,' I went on. 'Let's get moving. Angelo, you go with Chubby. Get round to Turtle Bay as quickly as you can. We'll meet you back there.

I ran towards the truck and Sherry got in beside me. The strange, hard look had returned to her face, but I said nothing.

When we reached Turtle Bay, we unloaded the truck and waited on the beach for Chubby and Angelo. Two hours later, they arrived.

We loaded the boat in an hour. At sunset, we were sailing out of Turtle Bay. Sherry and I sat under a cover, just in case anyone saw the boat. By the time the moon came up, we were out on the open sea.

11

Shark!

It was early morning when we reached the Old Men. Chubby and I took out some of the explosives. We buried[42] the rest under some palm trees.

Chubby and I worked with the explosives. It was a dangerous and difficult job. We had to work very carefully.

When we were ready, Sherry and I went down to the *Dawn Light*. We fixed the explosives carefully and came up. When we were back in the whaleboat, we connected the wires to a battery. Chubby turned the switch. Immediately, we felt a movement under the boat and the water swirled and bubbled.

'Right,' I said to Sherry. 'We can go down now. Let's hope we can find a way into *Dawn Light*.'

We were lucky. The explosion had torn off one of the big guns from the wooden ship. There was a hole big enough for us to swim through.

It was difficult to see through the muddy water. I pushed hard against a heavy piece of wood. It did not move. I tried again, pushing harder. Suddenly the wood broke. I fell forwards as pieces of wood and coral fell around me. In a few minutes we were inside the wreck.

We moved slowly forward and I shone my torch all around. We swam along the length of the ship until we came to the wooden wall of the hold[43]. Behind that wooden wall was the Tiger Throne, I was sure of it.

I looked at my watch. I turned to Sherry and pointed upwards. We had to get up to the surface. The air in our oxygen tanks was almost finished. Sherry and I swam out of the ship. Suddenly, as I looked up, I saw we were in great danger.

The explosion had killed hundreds of fish and the water was full of their blood. And a long black shadow was moving over our heads.

A shark! It had come into the pool to feed on the dead fish. As the shark turned, I saw its terrible mouth and hundreds of sharp teeth.

I looked at Sherry and pointed upwards again. Back to the boat! But we had to move slowly, as we went up, up, up to the surface. The shark was still feeding on the dead fish. I could see the bottom of the whaleboat now. Then I was up and Sherry was with me.

I turned and pushed Sherry up and over the side of the boat. Chubby and Angelo grabbed[44] her. She was safe!

I looked down again. At that moment, the shark saw me. I reached up, grabbed the side of the boat and pulled my legs up.

Just in time! A white shape burst through the water and

crashed against the boat. Then the shark swam under the boat and crashed against the other side.

Chubby stood up with the spear-gun[45] in his hand. As the terrible head rose out of the water, the spear exploded between the open jaws and the water went red. The shark fell back into the water of the pool – dead!

I pulled off my mask and smiled at Sherry.

'Time to go,' I said and Chubby turned the boat back into the channel and towards Old Men Island.

———

The next tide washed the blood and the dead fish out of the pool. There was no sign of sharks when we dived into the pool again.

'We must get into the hold,' I said. 'The best way in is through the deck. We'll use the explosives to blow a hole through the deck. Then we'll be able to pull up those boxes with ropes.'

Sherry and I dived down again to the wreck. I placed the explosives carefully and we came up again to the surface.

This time we didn't take any chances! We didn't want to meet any more sharks. After the explosion, we left the pool and went back to Old Men Island. The next tide would wash out the dead fish and it would be safe to go back.

At Old Men, we sat on the beach, we swam and we tried to relax. We all felt very excited. But I was worried. By now, Manny Resnick had found the ship's bell at Gull Island. I was sure of this. He had a big, fast ship and plenty of men to help him. We had to get the treasure out of the *Dawn Light* before he came looking for us. We had been lucky so far. I hoped that our luck would last.

Chubby stood up with the spear-gun in his hand.

12

Danger in the Air

It was the afternoon of the following day before we got into the hold. Inside the hold, we had another problem. Whenever we moved something, it stirred up mud and rotten wood. It was impossible to see anything. Our torches were useless. I searched with my hands. Suddenly my hands found a wooden box. It was very heavy. Sherry, Chubby and I dragged it into a net and used air-bags to lift it to the surface.

The tide was coming in as we got the box into the boat. We took the whaleboat back through the channel. The box was so heavy that we decided to open it on the beach at Old Men.

We used iron bars to break the box open. I saw at once that it wasn't the Tiger Throne. But it was treasure. The box was full of large gold plates! Sherry lifted one out and turned it over in her hands.

'It's beautiful!' she cried. 'And it must weigh over a kilo!' I took out another plate and looked at it carefully.

'We're rich,' I said, 'if we find the Throne or not.'

'These are just old plates,' Angelo said.

'They're old,' I said, 'but very valuable. They must be worth at least a hundred thousand pounds.'

'A hundred thousand pounds? That's crazy,' said Chubby.

'Crazy or not,' I said, 'it's true. We must search the ship more carefully.'

'But we can't see anything down there,' Chubby said. 'If we had a pump we could clean all the mud and rotten wood out of the hold. Then we would be able to see more clearly.'

'A pump! That's the answer,' I cried. 'Your uncle's got a pump, Chubby. We can borrow it and fix it up in the whaleboat.

Then we can use it to clean all the mud and rotten wood out of the hold.'

'OK,' Chubby said. 'I'll go back to St Mary's early tomorrow morning with Angelo. We'll get back here as soon as we can.'

'Good,' I said, 'and you can take the gold plates back with you. Bury them at Turtle Bay. If anything goes wrong we've got something that's worth money,' I told him.

Chubby and Angelo left early the next morning. After breakfast, Sherry and I left the caves and went down to the beach. We were swimming in the sea, when I heard a plane.

It was coming low over the island and flying directly towards us.

'Quick!' I shouted to Sherry. 'They mustn't see us. Get back to the palm trees!'

We ran out of the water, up the beach and into the palm trees. We covered ourselves with a broken branch. We were just in time. I looked up and saw a small plane. I had seen it before at St Mary's airport. It was used by rich tourists. I wondered who was paying for this trip.

The plane turned and I saw the passenger looking out of the window. It was Manny Resnick! The plane flew back and forwards over the beach. Then it turned and flew away. Sherry looked at me.

'What's going to happen now, Harry?' she said slowly. 'You know that man, don't you?'

'That was Manny Resnick,' I said. 'He's looking for us, that's certain.'

'Will we find the Tiger Throne before they find us, Harry?' Sherry whispered.

'I don't know,' I answered. 'Chubby may have some news. Let's wait until he gets back.'

Chubby did have news and it was bad.

'The *Mandrake*, the ship we saw in St Mary's harbour, has

The plane flew back and forwards over the beach.

been to Gull Island,' Chubby told us. 'Then it went back to St Mary's and the crew started asking questions.'

'Let's hope they didn't get too many answers,' I said. 'We've got to move quickly now. Have you brought the pump with you, Chubby?'

'Yes, Mr Harry,' Chubby said. 'I brought the pump and I brought this too.'

He had an automatic rifle in his hands.

13

'*Something Shone Brightly . . .*'

We used the pump to clean the muddy water out of the hold. On our second dive, we found some more boxes. The wooden boxes were rotten but they were held together by strips of iron.

I pulled away a piece of wood. There was some soft cloth behind the wood. As I pulled away the cloth, something shone brightly in the torchlight. I worked quickly and Sherry helped me. Suddenly, we were looking into the fierce face of a tiger. We had found the Tiger Throne!

The face was almost a metre wide. The mouth was open and we could see the golden teeth and tongue. There was a hole in the middle of the forehead, where the great diamond eye had been.

For a moment, Sherry and I could not move. We looked at the beautiful golden face. Then, very carefully, we began to pull it up out of the covering cloth.

We got the head up out of the water the next day. It weighed about 150 kilos. It was made of gold, about 25 centimetres thick.

Then we found the jewels. They had been pulled off the Throne and packed together in a smaller box. We carried everything up to the cave on the hillside. We opened the boxes there. The jewels were different colours – blue, yellow, red and green. I cleaned each one and held it up to the light.

It was Sherry who found the diamond eye. It was about the size of a chicken's egg and it flashed brightly. Sherry handed me the great diamond without a word. I got up and walked to the back of the cave. Very carefully, I fitted the diamond into the hole in the tiger's head. The animal seemed to come alive. The gold and the jewels shone in the light of our lamps.

'It's beautiful,' Sherry whispered. 'Beautiful and frightening too. I can't believe it's been under the sea for over a hundred years. What are we going to do with it, Harry?'

I thought for a moment and then I said, 'We still have to find the other pieces of the Throne. But tomorrow, we must get the head and the jewels away from here.'

I didn't tell the others, but I had made my plans already. I looked at the head again. 'It's safe for tonight. We'll sleep now. We'll go back to St Mary's at dawn tomorrow.'

14

Death on the Island

I woke up at about three o'clock in the morning. I dressed quickly and went to look at the tiger's head. The eye shone like a star in the light of my lamp.

I knew we must hide it now. I woke Chubby and together we

Very carefully, I fitted the diamond into the hole in the tiger's head.

carried the treasure down to the palm trees near the beach. We buried the beautiful things and the automatic rifle under the sand, near the place where we had hidden the explosives.

I felt happier now that the treasure was hidden. But I was still worried. I had to find out more about Sherry North. She had showed me that she loved me. But she sometimes looked at me in a strange way. I was sure there were many things she hadn't told me. I had to find out what they were.

I walked slowly to the highest point of the island and looked towards the sea. The sun was coming up now and I could see more clearly.

I gasped in horror. There, on the dark sea, was the *Mandrake*. Manny Resnick had found us already! As I watched, the *Mandrake* anchored and a small motor boat began moving towards the beach. I started to run down towards the caves. I fell two or three times as I ran down the steep path. I shouted to Chubby and Angelo.

'Quick, quick!' I cried. 'We've got visitors!'

'Manny Resnick?' Chubby asked.

'Right,' I said. 'Chubby, you get the rifle. Angelo, I want you to stay with Miss Sherry.'

'Go with Angelo,' I told Sherry quickly, 'and climb up to the highest point of the island. We'll come and join you there as soon as we've got the rifle. Remember – keep out of sight – Manny's a killer.'

'Yes, Harry, I know,' Sherry answered.

I watched them go and then I put a few things in a bag. I put on my belt, with its heavy knife. I went down towards the beach to meet Chubby. Suddenly, I heard shooting ahead of me. I stopped and waited. Chubby came running towards me, carrying the automatic rifle.

'Men got off the boat at two different places,' Chubby said. 'They saw me getting the gun.'

'Come on,' I called. 'We must get back to Sherry and Angelo.'

We hurried along the rough tracks, past some soft muddy ground, to the highest point of the island. Before we reached our meeting place, we heard machine-guns firing in front of us. We ran fast.

'Sherry!' I called. 'Sherry! Are you there, love?' There was no answer.

I looked down towards the beach and Gunfire Reef. Then I gasped in horror. The motor boat had turned and it was moving back towards the *Mandrake*. There was a woman sitting among the men on the boat.

'Is that Sherry?' I cried to Chubby. 'I can't see clearly.'

As we ran down towards the beach we heard more shots.

'They're still looking for us, Mr Harry,' Chubby said. 'The island must be full of men.'

'Never mind. We must find out what's happened to Sherry and Angelo.'

The ground was soft in front of us and we could see Sherry and Angelo's footprints.

And then we found Angelo. He had been shot three times and the sand was dark with his blood.

They had caught Sherry there. We could see the marks in the sand where she had tried to get away from the men.

I went back to Chubby and together we quickly covered Angelo's body with branches and sand. He would never enjoy his share of the treasure now.

Then we stood up and looked across the sea at the *Mandrake*. Now the whaleboat was also alongside her.

'They've taken our boat too, Mr Harry,' Chubby said.

'They've got Sherry and we're trapped.'

I got the binoculars out of my bag and looked through them. There were some people standing on the deck of the *Mandrake*. I saw Manny Resnick – just as I remembered him. And standing next to him was the blonde girl who had called herself Sherry North.

'Look, Mr Harry, there's more of them getting into the

*He had been shot three times and the sand was dark
with his blood.*

whaleboat,' Chubby whispered. 'They're coming back towards the beach.'

'Right,' I answered. 'We've got to move fast. They've got a lot of men and lots of guns. And they're looking for us! We've got one gun and we need another.

'You stay here, Chubby – and keep the rifle. But don't use it unless you have to.'

The whaleboat had nearly reached the beach. There were ten men on board, all carrying rifles.

I ran back to the muddy ground. I had to find the group of men who were on the island. I ran quickly round the soft ground. Then I stopped and hid behind some trees. I waited quietly.

As I had hoped, the men were walking towards the muddy ground and they were not walking together. One of the men was coming slowly towards me. When he was near enough I stood up suddenly. I threw my knife and it went deep into his throat. He dropped to the ground without making a sound.

I pulled out the knife and cleaned it in the sand. It took the man's machine-gun and moved back into the shelter of the trees. Then I heard the noise of the automatic rifle. A machine-gun answered and then there was silence. I moved quickly towards the sound of the firing. The first man I met was running so fast that he nearly knocked me over. Six others were following him. They had dropped their guns and were running away from Chubby in terror.

I raised the machine-gun and I fired at them until they lay still.

I ran up the track and found Chubby.

'Sorry, Mr Harry, I had to fire at them,' he grinned. 'They were just standing there. I got two and the others ran away.'

'They won't run again,' I said. 'But remember there are more men landing on the island. And Manny Resnick has still got Sherry.'

As we stood there, I heard a voice coming clearly across the water of the bay. It was Manny Resnick's voice. He was using a loudhailer[46].

'Harry Fletcher! We've got something to show you. Why don't you come down to the beach? You can see it better from there.'

'Don't go, Mr Harry,' Chubby whispered. 'They'll catch us.'

'I don't think so,' I replied. 'Look, the whaleboat is going back. There's no one left on the island but us. And they've got Sherry. Come on, I'm going down.'

I took the rifle from Chubby.

'I'm going to walk onto the beach,' I told him. 'But you hide behind the trees. I want them to think that I'm alone.'

I stopped under the palms near the beach. Manny and the blonde were on the deck of the *Mandrake*. Then two men brought Sherry up onto the deck and held her between them.

I looked at her through my binoculars. Her face was bruised and bloody. There was blood on her blue shirt. One of her hands was covered with a white cloth. It was red with blood.

I had the rifle. For one moment, I was so angry that I thought of killing Resnick. But if I killed Manny Resnick, they would kill Sherry immediately. Resnick put the loudhailer to his mouth and began to speak again.

'Good afternoon, Harry. Glad you could join us. We've been asking the lady a few questions. But she doesn't know all the answers. She doesn't know where the treasure is, so she can't give us any more help.

'Tell us where the treasure is, Harry, and you can have her back. If you don't tell us, we'll kill her.'

Sherry looked towards me. She shook her head. She didn't want me to tell them. The blonde walked up to her and hit her hard on the face. Manny laughed.

'Harry, you've got until midday tomorrow to think about it and give us your decision!'

Sherry was pulled roughly back into the cabin and the others followed.

I walked slowly back to the palm trees and waited for Chubby to join me.

'We've got work to do, my friend,' I told him. 'And we've got to work fast!'

15

The Plan Succeeds

I made Chubby repeat the instructions I gave him. We could not make any mistakes now.

We worked quickly and by 3 a.m. I was ready for my trip to the *Mandrake*. It was a long way to swim. But at last I reached the dark shadow of the ship. I fixed the explosives to the side of the *Mandrake*. In a few hours' time, the *Mandrake* and everyone aboard would be blown to pieces.

Chubby was waiting for me on the beach. He helped me to walk back to the palm trees. I fell down on the sand and slept.

Chubby woke me. I was ready immediately. I gave Chubby the rifle. We shook hands, but said nothing. That would have been unlucky.

When Chubby had gone, I went down to the beach and shouted. Almost at once, the deck of the *Mandrake* was full of men. Manny and the blonde were there too.

Some men jumped into the motor boat and it headed towards the beach. A few minutes later, I was on the deck of the *Mandrake* with all the guns pointing at me.

'Well, Harry Fletcher – or should I say Harry Bruce?' said

Manny with a smile. 'And now we're using our real names, this is Miss Lorna Page. I think you have met before.'

I stared at the blonde girl standing by his side. She smiled and I hated her.

'Let's get down to business, Harry,' Manny said. 'You've got the Tiger Throne.'

'Part of it,' I replied. 'Only the head. It's gold all right. It weighs about 150 kilos.'

'That's not all,' said Lorna Page greedily. 'You've got the jewels. The girl told us.'

So Sherry had told them everything she knew. They must have hurt her badly.

'Yes, I've got the jewels . . .' I replied.

'And the big diamond – the Eye of the Tiger? You've got that too?' said Lorna Page.

'Yes. But I'm the only one who knows where that is. You want the diamond. Well, I want Sherry North.'

'Sherry North?' Manny repeated with a laugh. 'You're a bigger fool than I thought, Harry. We don't want the girl any more. You can have her.'

'Then you must give me back the whaleboat, with fuel and water.' I stopped for a moment and then I said, 'And I want to keep the tiger's head.'

'You're getting too greedy, Harry,' Manny replied.

'You take the diamond,' I said, 'and all the other jewels. They're worth millions. Just let me keep the head.'

'You'll take your life and think yourself lucky,' Manny answered. His eyes were cold and hard. I knew then that they would kill me when they had found the treasure.

'OK,' I said. 'I haven't any choice. But I'm taking the girl.'

'Of course, Harry, of course,' Manny said with a smile.

They brought Sherry up on deck and I looked at her in horror. Her face was black and blue where they had hit her. I took her in my arms.

'Thank God, Harry,' she whispered. 'Thank God you came.'

I turned my head. I did not want the others to see the hate in my eyes.

'Right, there's nothing to wait for,' I said. 'Let's get back to the island.'

Sherry sat close to me in the motor boat. Lorna Page and Manny Resnick sat at the back of the boat.

'They're going to kill us, Harry,' she whispered.

'What happened to your hand?' I asked her.

'It was the girl, Lorna Page. She pulled out my finger nails. It was terrible, terrible . . .'

I held her close. 'It's all right now,' I told her.

'OK, Harry,' said Manny, as we stood on the beach. 'My men are bringing the whaleboat to the island. When you've shown us the treasure, you and the girl can go.'

Lorna Page smiled. She knew that Manny was not going to let us go.

'You go first, Harry,' Manny said and we all began to move across the beach. Two of the men stayed on the boats. I looked at my watch quickly and walked on. After a while I looked round and then stopped.

'Tell your men to dig here, Manny,' I said. Four men began to dig quickly.

'Sherry's hurt,' I said to Manny. 'She needs to sit down in the shade.'

Manny nodded. Two of his men walked with us to the trees, about forty metres away. There was no sign of Chubby but that was part of my plan.

The men went on digging. Then one of them gave a shout. They all stood round the hole, shouting excitedly.

'Be careful. Use the ropes to get it out,' Manny said. 'Let me see.'

He jumped into the hole and Lorna Page stood at the edge, looking down greedily.

It was perfect[47]. I raised my hand to my head. This was the signal I had planned with Chubby. Then I grabbed Sherry and jumped backwards into a shallow hole that Chubby and I had dug earlier in the morning.

'Now, Chubby, now!' I whispered. I threw myself on top of Sherry and covered her ears with my hands. There was an enormous explosion. I was deafened by the noise and blinded with dust. My hands felt for the machine-gun I had buried in the sand. I pulled out the gun and fired at the guards. They died at once.

Then I went to the place where the others had been.

All of Manny's men were dead. The body of Lorna Page lay on the sand. Her dead eyes stared up at the blue sky. The torn body of Manny Resnick lay at the bottom of the hole. Everything was quiet.

And then Chubby was running down the beach to meet us.

'Quick, Mr Harry, we've got to get back to the whaleboat. Resnick's men are trying to sink it!' Chubby was shouting.

I could hear the shots now. I threw down the machine-gun and grabbed the rifle from Chubby.

'You stay here with Sherry,' I told Chubby. But Chubby ran after me. He wanted to get back to his boat.

Resnick's men were in the motor boat. One of them was shooting at the whaleboat, trying to sink it. I raised the rifle and fired at them. Then there was another shot and Chubby fell at my feet.

'Get him, Mr Harry. Get him before he gets you,' Chubby whispered. I fired again, but the motor boat had almost reached the *Mandrake*. I looked at my watch then down at Chubby. Blood was pouring out of a hole in his chest.

Sherry knelt beside him and held his head in her arms.

'I'll never be rich, Miss Sherry,' Chubby whispered. 'But you and Mr Harry will be all right. Take good care of her, Mr Harry.'

I was holding his hand when he died. Sherry and I looked at each other with tears in our eyes.

There was a strange roaring sound from the sea.

'My God, look, Harry!' Sherry cried.

The *Mandrake* and the motor boat had both gone. In their place a great fountain of water showed white against the blue sky. Then the water fell back into the sea and all was quiet.

16

The Last Problem

Sherry and I spent the next three weeks at Turtle Bay. I had a meeting with the President and we talked for more than two hours.

They were not happy weeks. We were sad about Chubby and Angelo. Was the treasure worth the deaths of those two good friends?

Sherry's nails began to grow again. Our bodies became stronger, but we had too many bad memories to be happy.

One evening we sat together by the sea. I knew it was time to tell Sherry what I had planned. My plan would not work without her. I told her what I had decided.

I had put all the treasure into a large coffin[48]. Sherry was going to fly to Zurich. She would be waiting there, dressed in black, when the coffin arrived. She would say it contained the body of her husband. No one would open a coffin. I knew people in Zurich who would buy the treasure and ask no questions.

Sherry listened and said nothing. I took out a plane ticket from my pocket and handed it to her.

'But this is for a flight tomorrow!' she said.

'That's right. I've made all the arrangements.'

'But what about you, Harry? When shall I see you?'

'I'll get to Zurich two days after you. My plane lands at 1.30 pm. Be there to meet me.'

As we drove to St Mary's the next day, Sherry did not look happy. She tried to tell me something. But what she said did not make sense.

'Harry, if anything happens to us . . . you know, nothing lasts for ever, does it? I mean . . .'

'What do you mean?' I said.

'No, it's nothing. It's just that – well, if anything happens . . .' she said no more.

I watched her get onto the plane. She did not wave to me or look back. I completed the flight arrangements for getting the coffin to Zurich. I stayed the night at the old hotel by the harbour. The next day, I left St Mary's.

As I was a day early, there was no one to meet me at Zurich Airport. I booked a flight back to St Mary's for 1.20 pm the following day. Then I went and had a long talk to the pretty girl on the Information Desk.

'Can you help me?' I asked, when I had explained everything to her.

'Yes, sir, I will,' she said with a smile.

I went and stayed the night in a small hotel. At midday, the following day, I went back to the airport. I sat in the café, reading a newspaper and watching people arrive.

No one would know me. I was wearing a suit that was too big for me. My hair was grey and I was wearing glasses. When I had looked in the mirror, I didn't know who I was!

Just after one o'clock, I saw Sherry North. She was wearing a black leather coat and dark glasses. But she was not alone. There were five men walking behind her. They walked quietly and looked around at everyone. They stopped and one of the men gave orders. Sherry listened quietly.

I knew I was in big trouble. Those men were policemen and

they all had guns. But I wasn't going to run now! I had a plan and I was going to stick to it[49]. Then four of the men walked to the passenger arrival gates. At that moment, the departure of my plane was announced.

I walked to the Information Desk. At first, the girl didn't recognise me, but then she laughed.

'You certainly look different today,' she said. 'Go to the last phone-booth over by the departure gate.'

I walked slowly over to the phone booth. It seemed a very long way. I lifted up the phone and pretended to speak. Then I heard the announcement.

'Will Miss Sherry North come to the Information Desk. Miss Sherry North to the Desk, please.'

Through the glass door of the phone booth, I saw Sherry go over to the Information Desk. The girl at the desk pointed to the phone-booth next to mine and Sherry walked towards it.

As soon as she was in the phone-booth, I moved to the door and opened it.

'OK,' I said, 'turn round, Policewoman – whoever you are!'

She turned and looked at me in horror.

'Yes, it's me, stupid old Harry,' I said. 'Tell me, what happened to the real Sherry North?'

'She was killed. We found the body.'

'I knew it,' I said. 'And Manny Resnick laughed at me. He knew who you were, because he had already killed Sherry. He called me a fool. He was right, wasn't he?'

She stood looking at me, but said nothing.

'So when Sherry North was killed,' I went on, 'the police decided you would take her place. They hoped someone would come and lead them to the killer. I heard you phoning that night in Falmer. You were telling the police I had arrived. And they told you what to do. You did it well, didn't you?'

'If you knew all this, why did you take me with you?' she said.

She turned and looked at me in horror.

'I wasn't sure at first,' I replied. 'And by the time I was sure, I was in love with you. And at one time, I thought you loved me too.'

'I'm a policewoman,' she said quickly. 'And you're a thief.'

'Yes, I was once. But that was a long time ago.'

'But you've got the Throne – the Tiger Throne.'

'No, I haven't,' I said. 'That coffin's full of sand.'

'Then where's the Throne?'

'It's where it belongs, with the President of St Mary's,' I replied.

'You've given the treasure to St Mary's?' she said in surprise. 'You've given it up, but you still came here? Why, Harry? Why?'

'To give you a choice,' I said quietly. 'And you've got to make that choice now. My plane leaves in a few minutes. If no one stops me, I'm going to get on it. I'll be at Turtle Bay tomorrow, waiting for you.'

'But they'll come after you, Harry . . .'

'No. Once I'm on St Mary's, I'll be safe. Goodbye,' I said. 'I'm going to be lonely out there at Turtle Bay without you.'

I turned and walked slowly to the departure gate. No one stopped me and I didn't look back.

I sat in the plane thinking. How long would it be before she flew out to St Mary's? I still had a lot to tell her. I had promised the President that I'd get the rest of the Tiger Throne up from the wreck. The Throne would belong to the people of St Mary's. In return, I'd get a new boat. I would be able to live well. And I still had the gold plates hidden in Turtle Bay. No one knew about them.

Then I realised that I didn't even know her real name. That would be the first thing I would ask her when I met her at St Mary's airport.

I sat back and closed my eyes. I thought about the future. It was going to be good.

Points for Understanding

1

1 Who is Harry Fletcher?
2 What is *Wave Dancer*?
3 Who are Chubby and Angelo?
4 Why was Harry Fletcher a happy man?
5 What two questions did Guthrie ask Harry Fletcher?
6 What was Materson planning to do?
7 Who did Materson not want on board the *Wave Dancer*?
8 Where was Turtle Bay?
9 Why did Harry feel angry and unhappy?
10 Guthrie reminded Harry Fletcher of his past life.
    (a)   What kind of life had Harry lived in the past?
    (b)   Did Harry want to go back to his past life?

2

1 What did Harry do when he was seventeen?
2 How did Harry learn to shoot and kill?
3 One day, in the middle of Africa, Harry decided what he wanted. What did he want?
4 What crime did Harry plan in South Africa?
5 Who did he get to help him? Did the crime succeed?
6 Harry told Manny Resnick that he had finished with crime. What was Manny Resnick's reply?
7 What did Harry do with the money from his crime?
8 Why did Harry Fletcher like Jimmy North?
9 Why was it dangerous to sail towards the African coast?
10 Why did Harry agree to go there?
11 How could Harry save Materson time and money?
12 What did Jimmy North begin to say?
13 Why did Jimmy North not finish what he was saying?
14 What two things happened on the third day?
15 Why did Harry begin to feel excited?

3

1 When could a ship go through Gunfire Break?
2 How long could a ship stay in the pool behind Gunfire Break?
3 Was there another way out of the deep pool?
4 Why did Harry refuse to go through Gunfire Break?
5 What did Harry see written on the side of the sledge?
6 Jimmy North found something heavy. Why could Harry not see what the object was?
7 What happened when Harry Fletcher went towards the object to have a look at it?

4

1 How did Harry get back on board *Wave Dancer*?
2 Why did Harry have to kill Materson and Guthrie?
3 What happened when Harry fired his last bullet?
4 How did Harry kill Guthrie?
5 Where was Harry when he woke up?
6 What did Harry do with the bundle?
7 Who found Harry?

5

1 Who was Judith and how was she able to help Harry?
2 How did Harry make a lot of money?
3 Why would Harry go back to Gull Island one day?
4 A woman at the Hilton Hotel wanted to meet Harry.
   (a) Who did she say she was?
   (b) What did she want from Harry?
   (c) Did Harry tell her everything he knew?
5 What did the woman say Jimmy North had been looking for?
6 Did Harry agree to help the woman?

6

1 Why was Harry sure the object was not a missile?
2 Why did Harry turn off the electrical power?
3 As he unwrapped the bundle, what did Harry see on Sherry North's face for one second?

67

4 What letters did Harry see on the old ship's bell?
5 Why could Sherry not light the stove?
6 What tap did you have to turn to light the stove?
7 What would happen if the taps were not turned off?
8 Why did Judith go to *Wave Dancer*?
9 Harry called at the Hilton Hotel.
    (a) What did the receptionist tell him?
    (b) Why was he suddenly afraid for Judith?
10 What happened when Judith got on board *Wave Dancer*?

7

1 Why was Harry Fletcher back where he started?
2 Harry was now sure that the blonde girl was not Jimmy North's sister. But there were many things he did not know about her. What were they?
3 How did Harry know Manson's address?
4 How did he know Jimmy North's address?
5 What did Harry decide to do?
6 A girl opened the door of Seaview Cottage. Who did she say she was and how did she know Harry's name?
7 What did Harry tell this girl?
8 Harry woke up later in the night. What did he hear?
9 Harry found two words underlined in a letter.
    (a) Where had Harry heard the words before?
    (b) What letters had Harry seen on the ship's bell?
10 Where had the *Dawn Light* been wrecked?
11 What had Jimmy North been looking for?

8

1 What was the Tiger Throne?
2 How many boxes were put on board the *Dawn Light*?
3 Why did the blonde girl and her friend, Manson, believe that the *Dawn Light* had sunk near Gull Island?
4 Would they find the treasure there?
5 How did Harry and Sherry North plan to find the treasure?
6 When Sherry saw Turtle Bay, she was amazed.
    (a) What did Sherry think of Turtle Bay?
    (b) What did Harry notice once or twice in her eyes?
    (c) Why was Harry happier than he had ever been before?

7 Where did they make their camp on Old Men Island?
8 Why could they not work in the pool all the time?
9 Who did Harry think would be back soon?
10 How would Harry know when they arrived at St Mary's?

9

1 Chubby had found an old coin.
    (a)   What was on the coin?
    (b)   Where had Chubby found it?
2 What pattern did they see on the china plate?
3 Why would they need explosives?
4 Harry wanted to have three things.
    (a)   What were the three things Harry wanted?
    (b)   What would he have to do to get them?

10

1 Harry looked at the ship through his binoculars.
    (a)   Who was the girl standing on the ship?
    (b)   Who was the man?
    (c)   What could this man do to Harry?
2 Why was Angelo ready to kill both the girl and the man?
3 What did Harry notice about Sherrys' face as he got into the truck beside her?
4 Why did Harry and Sherry sit under cover as they sailed out of Turtle Bay?

11

1 How did Harry and Sherry get inside the wreck?
2 What did Harry think was behind the wooden wall of the hold?
3 What danger were they in on the way back to the surface?
4 Why did they not go back down to the wreck after the explosion?
5 Why did they have to get the treasure out of the *Dawn Light* as quickly as possible?

12

1 What problem did they have when they were inside the hold?
2 What did they find inside the box?

3 Why did Chubby and Angelo go back to St Mary's?
4 What were Chubby and Angelo going to bury at Turtle Bay?
5 Who was the passenger in the plane?
6 Chubby did have news and it was bad.
   (a)   Where had the *Mandrake* been?
   (b)   What did the crew of the *Mandrake* do when they got back to St Mary's?
7 What two things did Chubby bring back from St Mary's?

13

1 We had found the Tiger Throne.
   (a)   What was the head of the tiger made of?
   (b)   Why was there a hole in the middle of the forehead?
2 Where did they find the jewels?
3 How big was the diamond eye?
4 What did Harry not tell the others?

14

1 Who helped Harry to hide the treasure? Where did they hide it? What else did they hide?
2 Why was Harry sure that Sherry had not told him everything about herself?
3 What did Harry see from the highest point of the island? What did he do?
4 What orders did Harry give to Chubby and Angelo?
5 There was a woman in the motor boat. Who did Harry think it was?
6 Why would Angelo never enjoy his share of the treasure?
7 How did Harry get hold of a machine-gun?
8 What did Manny Resnick ask Harry to do?
9 Why did Harry tell Chubby to keep out of sight?
10 Why could Harry not kill Manny Resnick?
11 Why was Sherry not able to tell them where the treasure was hidden?
12 What offer did Manny Resnick make to Harry?

15

1 Who were Harry Bruce and Lorna Page?
2 Why was Harry sure they were going to kill him?

3 What had Lorna Page done to Sherry to make her talk?
4 Why did Harry raise his hand to his head?
5 Why did Harry grab Sherry and jump into a shallow hole?
6 What happened next?
7 How did Chubby die?
8 What happened to the *Mandrake*?

16

1 Harry told Sherry his plan. What was his plan?
2 On the way to the airport, Sherry tried to tell Harry something.
   What do you think she wanted to tell him?
3 What arrangements did Harry make at the airport at Zurich?
4 Who did Harry see walking behind Sherry?
5 How did Harry manage to speak to Sherry alone?
6 What had happened to the real Sherry North?
7 Where was the Tiger Throne?
8 Harry gave the woman a choice. What was the choice?
9 What was the deal Harry had made with the President?
10 What had Harry kept hidden in Turtle Bay?
11 What would be the first question that Harry would ask the
   woman when he met her at St Mary's airport?

Glossary

1 **crew** (page 4)
   the people who work on a boat.
2 **wharf** (page 4)
   the part of a harbour where boats tie up so that people can get off and on.
3 **cabin** (page 4)
   a room in a boat below the deck where people can sit and sleep in comfort.

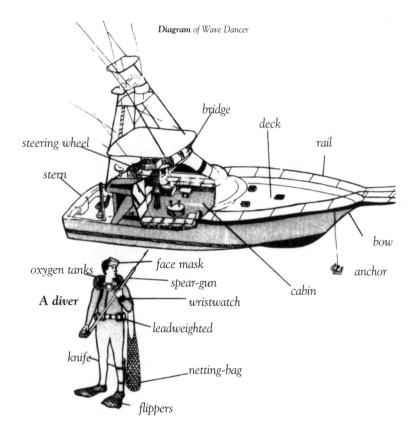

Diagram *of Wave Dancer*

bridge

deck

steering wheel

rail

stern

bow

oxygen tanks

face mask

anchor

spear-gun

A diver

cabin

wristwatch

leadweighted

knife

netting-bag

flippers

4   **her** (page 4)
    pronoun referring to the *Wave Dancer*. Boats and ships are
    usually referred to by the feminine pronouns – 'she' and 'her'.

5   **diving** (page 4)
    this is a story about valuable treasure, silver and jewels, which is
    lying in the wreck of a ship which was sunk in a storm. In order
    to find the treasure and get it up to the surface, divers have to go
    down deep under the water. If divers want to go down deep and
    stay for a long time, they have to have tanks of oxygen fixed to
    their backs. See the illustrations on pages 36 and 43.

6   **break the law** (page 7)
    to break the law is to commit a crime – to do something which is
    illegal.

7   **security firm** (page 7)
    a company which guards valuables and property against thieves.

8   **false passport** (page 7)
    when criminals try to go from one country to another, they can
    be caught because their names and photographs are on their
    passports. In order to avoid being caught like this, criminals often
    use false passports which do not show their real names and they
    are photographed wearing a disguise.

9   **instructions, not orders** (page 8)
    you follow instructions – they tell you what to do, usually in a
    polite way. You obey orders – they are often not given in a polite
    way.

10 **offshore** (page 8)
    part of the sea which is near to land.

11 **river mouth** (page 8)
    where a river runs into the sea.

12 **reef** (page 8)
    coral is made by the bodies of millions of very small sea animals
    and is dropped onto the bottom of the sea. Over many years, the
    coral builds up until it reaches the surface of the water.
        A long line of coral is called a reef. A coral reef can be seen at
    sea by the huge waves which break over the top. Coral is hard
    like rock, and its edges are sharp. It is a very dangerous place for
    ships.
        Sometimes, the coral builds up into a circular wall and the
    water inside the wall of coral is called a lagoon. An opening in
    the wall of coral is sometimes called a break.

13 **bridge** (page 8)
    the upper part of a boat where the captain stands and gives
    orders.

14 *anchored* (page 10)

when a boat wants to stay in one place when it is out at sea, it drops an anchor – a heavy weight which lies on the bottom of the sea.

15 *tide* (page 11)

the tide is the movement of water in a sea or an ocean. This movement happens about every twelve hours. The water in the ocean rises and falls. The time when the water is at its highest, is called high water, or high tide.

16 *sledge* (page 11)

usually a sledge goes over snow. In this story, the sledge is like a small boat with a flat bottom. A rope is fixed from the boat to the sledge behind it. The person on the sledge is able to control it so that it moves under the surface of the water.

17 *marker* (page 12)

a marker is something which floats on top of the water. It is brightly coloured and can be easily seen. There is a weight (an anchor) fixed to the marker so that it cannot move about in the water. The marker shows where something is lying on the bottom of the sea.

18 *steady* (page 12)

to hold a boat steady at sea is to try to keep it in one place without an anchor.

19 *air-bag* (page 12)

an air-bag is used to lift a heavy object from the bottom of the sea. When the air-bag is flat it is fixed under the object. Then air is pumped into the bag and it moves slowly to the surface bringing the heavy object up with it.

20 *set the automatic pilot on a course* (page 16)

the automatic pilot is an electronic instrument which can be used to guide a boat. When the automatic pilot is set you do not have to steer the boat yourself. The automatic pilot can tell if the waves or the wind have changed the way the boat is going. If this happens, the automatic pilot moves the steering wheel of the boat so that it goes in the right direction.

21 *bundle* (page 17)

something wrapped up in a covering of cloth is often called a bundle.

22 *whaleboat* (page 17)

a roughly built boat. It cannot go very fast and it is not very comfortable.

23 *scar* (page 18)

a mark on the skin left after a cut or a wound has healed.

24 **fishing season** (page 18)
the times of the year when fishermen go out in their boats to catch fish. During certain months of each year, fishermen do not go out to catch fish. During these months, the young fish are given time to grow larger.

25 **smuggle** (page 18)
to take things into a country without paying any taxes on them.

26 **trust** (page 20)
to trust someone is to believe that they are honest and they tell the truth.

27 **ship's bell** (page 22)
at one time every ship carried a large bell. This bell was rung to tell one group of seamen when to finish work and another group of seamen when to begin.

28 **crest** (page 22)
the bell has a design on the metal to show who owned the ship. Important people often put their crests, or special designs, onto their valuable things. Crests can have pictures of people or animals on them.

29 **seasick** (page 22)
some people feel unwell on boats. In bad weather, when boats move about in the water, people feel seasick.

30 **stove** (page 22)
a gas cooker on a boat. The gas is kept in a cylinder. There is a tap on the cylinder. When the tap is shut, the gas cannot get out of the cylinder. But when the tap is opened, the gas can get out into the air. The stove can then be lit with a match. It is dangerous to leave the tap open when the stove is not being used.

31 **insurance agent** (page 26)
you insure a house, a boat or a car by paying money to an insurance agent. If there is an accident, the insurance agent has to pay the money to replace the thing which is damaged or destroyed. Insurance agents have to insure with large companies so that they have enough money to pay for anything which might happen. Harry Fletcher's insurance agent cheated by not paying money to insure with a larger company. So Harry Fletcher did not get any money to buy a new boat.

32 **hire** (page 27)
when you hire a car, you pay to have it for a short time only – a day, a week or a month.

33　*files* (page 28)
the papers on a subject are kept together in a folder called a file.

34　*photocopied* (page 29)
a photocopier is a machine which makes copies of anything written or drawn on paper. The words or plans have been photocopied from a book.

35　**Indian Mutiny** (page 31)
in 1857, Indian soldiers rebelled against their English officers. During the Mutiny, robbers were able to steal many valuable things from palaces and temples.

36　*plan of the ship* (page 31)
a drawing showing the different parts of the ship.

37　*camping equipment* (page 32)
things needed when anyone goes camping – tents, blankets, pots for cooking, etc.

38　*netting-bag* (page 35)
a bag made of knotted string. Netting-bags are used by divers to hold anything which they find under the water. The net holds the things in the bag and lets the sea water run out.

39　*explosives* (page 37)
examples of explosives are dynamite and nitroglycerine. An explosive is set off under water by an electrical charge.

40　*delighted* (page 38)
very pleased.

41　*binoculars* (page 39)
binoculars enable anyone looking through them to see things at a distance more clearly.

42　*bury* (page 40)
something is buried when it is put in the ground and covered over with earth.

43　*hold* (page 41)
the part of the ship below the decks where goods are kept.

44　*grab* (page 41)
to grab someone is to catch hold of them quickly and hold them tightly.

45　*spear-gun* (page 42)
a weapon used by a diver to hunt fish under the water. See the illustration on page 43.

46　*loud hailer* (page 54)
when you speak through a loud hailer, your voice can be heard clearly at a distance.

47 *perfect* (page 58)
    Harry Fletcher had made a plan to kill Manny Resnick and his
    gang. The plan worked when Manny Resnick jumped down into
    the hole and so it was perfect.
48 *coffin* (page 60)
    the box in which a dead body is placed before it is buried.
49 *stick to it* (page 62)
    Harry has made a plan. He is in danger, but he will carry out his
    plan. He is going to stick to it.

Rage
Power of the Sword
The Angels Weep
The Burning Shore
Cry Wolf
The Dark of the Sun
The Diamond Hunters
Eagle in the Sky
A Falcon Flies
Gold Mine
Hungry as the Sea
The Leopard Hunts in Darkness
Men of Men
Shout at the Devil
The Sound of Thunder
A Sparrow Falls
The Sunbird
When the Lion Feeds
Wild Justice